PRECIOUS MOMENTS

Let's Be Thankful

By Matt Mitter

Illustrated by Samuel J. Butcher

A GOLDEN BOOK • NEW YORK

Golden Books Publishing Company, Inc., New York, New York 10106

Long ago the first Thanksgiving dinner
Was prepared . . .

$\mathcal{B}$y neighbors giving thanks to God
for blessings they had shared.

We have Thanksgiving still
As they did centuries before,

Reminding me of all the things
That I am thankful for.

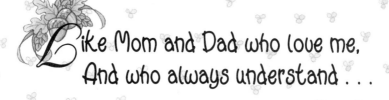

*Like Mom and Dad who love me,
And who always understand . . .*

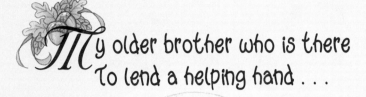

My older brother who is there
To lend a helping hand . . .

My friends who help me get back up
When my plans don't succeed,

And friends who give a gentle push
When that is all I need.

I'm thankful for my teachers, too,
Who help to stretch my mind.

REPORT CARD
Kindness .. A
Mercy ... A
Love ... A
Faithfulness A

teacher

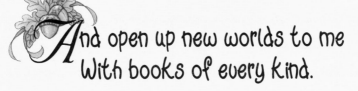

And open up new worlds to me
With books of every kind.

I'm thankful for the time I have
To play games with my team.

And thankful for the time I have
Alone—to think and dream.

And music—I'm so thankful
for the songs that we can sing . . .

And the music that surrounds us
Made by every living thing!

I'm thankful for this world which God
Has given to us all,

For the endless wonders in it—
  Every creature great and small . . .

The creatures living in the forests
Jungles, fields, and seas . . .

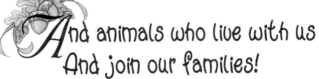

And animals who live with us
And join our families!

I'm thankful for the gentle breeze
That rustles through my hair,

And soft cool showers that
feed the flowers
Which pop up everywhere!

I'm thankful for the vegetables
And fruits that Nature brings.

With which we make Thanksgiving pies
And other tasty things!

Thanksgiving lets us praise what God
Has given me and you.
And joins us all in peace and love—
I'm thankful for that, too!